Ruby Gets Crafty

Grosset & Dunlap
An Imprint of Penguin Group (USA) Inc.

From an episode of the animated television series *Max & Ruby*.
Series © 2011–2012 M&R V Productions Ltd. All rights reserved.

Max & Ruby © Rosemary Wells. Licensed by Nelvana Limited. NELVANA is a registered trademark of Nelvana Limited.
CORUS is a trademark of Corus Entertainment Inc. All rights reserved. Published in 2013 by Grosset & Dunlap, a division of Penguin Young Readers Group,
345 Hudson Street, New York, New York 10014. GROSSET & DUNLAP is a trademark of Penguin Group (USA) Inc. Manufactured in China.

ISBN 978-0-448-46742-9   10 9 8 7 6 5 4 3 2 1

ALWAYS LEARNING   PEARSON

"Let's make a memory poster," said Ruby.

"Great idea!" said Louise.

"Let's think of our favorite memories," said Ruby.

"Giddyap, giddyap! Cloppity, cloppity, clop!" said Max to his horse, Silver.

"Our camping trip last summer was fun," said Louise.

"Why don't we put a campfire in the first square?" asked Ruby.

"With marshmallows!" said Louise.

"Hiyo, Silver!" said Max.

Louise and Ruby thought about what to do for the next square on their memory poster.

"Giddyap, Silver!" said Max, leaving Ruby's room.

"Bye, Max!" said Ruby and Louise.

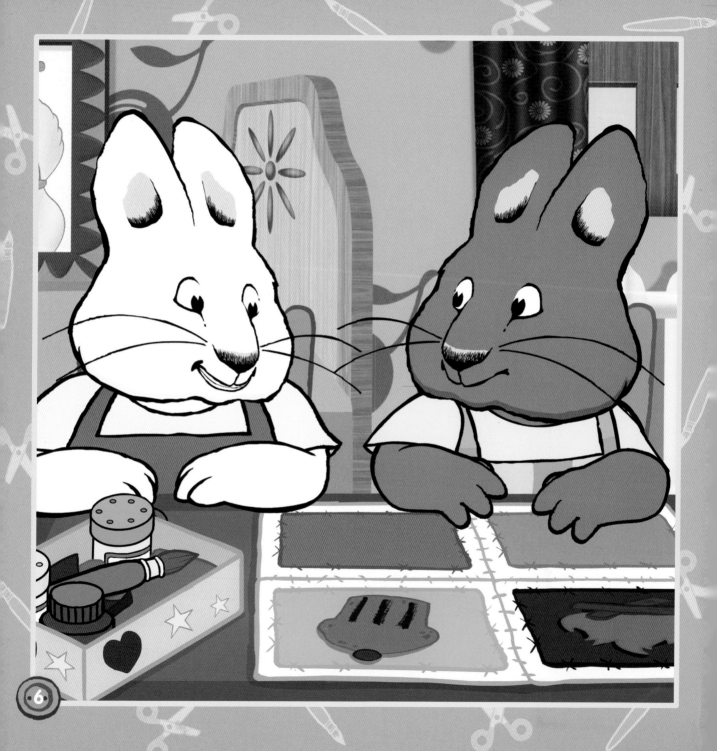

"Remember when we baked cupcakes at Grandma's house?" asked Ruby.

"That was so much fun!" said Louise.

Louise drew a cupcake in the second square.

"That's pretty, but it needs something else," said Ruby.

 Meanwhile, Max made Silver jump over all the mountain streams and boulders.

"Giddyap!" said Max, as he went back to Ruby's room.

"Go away, Max," said Ruby. "You'll knock something over."
"Neeeiiighhhh!" said Max. "Cloppity, cloppity, clop!"

Silver's head bumped the glitter jar.

"Oh no!" said Ruby.

"But look, Ruby," said Louise. "The glitter is perfect on our cupcake icing!"

"Giddyap!" said Max, going back to his room.

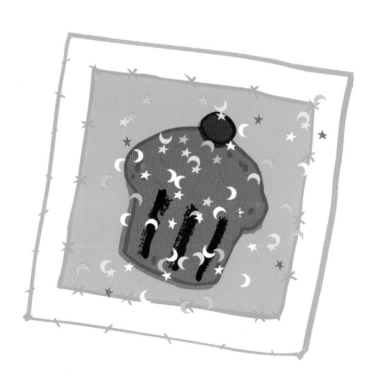

Ruby and Louise thought about what to do for the third square on their memory poster.

"Do you remember ballet class?" asked Louise.

"Of course!" said Ruby. She twirled around in a *pirouette*.

"How about we use this tissue paper for a ballerina's tutu?" asked Louise.

"That's too pink!" said Ruby. "Let's find my old tutu and match the color."

Meanwhile, Max found a box of windup ladybugs in his room. The ladybugs made Silver rear and jump.

When Max and Silver went back to Ruby's room, Silver would not be quiet.

"Calm down!" said Max to Silver.

Silver still would not calm down. Max had to pull on the reins. Silver ripped a piece out of Ruby's old tutu. "Let's use this piece for our poster," said Ruby.

"What should we put in the fourth memory square?"
asked Ruby.
"How about the tulips we planted in Grandma's garden?"
said Louise.

"Perfect!" said Ruby. "Let's open different-colored paints."

Max practiced roping while Silver rested in his stall.

Max went into Ruby's room.

Swoosh! went the rope. The paint spilled onto the table, the floor, and Ruby's paws.

"Oh no!" said Louise.

"But look—we can make paw-print art for our fourth square," said Ruby.

"What a great idea!" said Louise.

"We made a beautiful memory poster," said Ruby.
"Even with Max, Silver, and the rope!" said Louise.
"Hiyo, Silver!" said Max.